HAROLD BERSON

Charles and Claudine

ADAPTED FROM AN OLD FRENCH TALE

Macmillan Publishing Co., Inc.

New York

Collier Macmillan Publishers

London

Once, in a small village in France, there lived the woodcutter Antoine, his wife Antoinette, and their thirteen children. Antoine and Antoinette were very happy the day their fourteenth child, a daughter, was born. But they now had to find a godmother—and that was not going to be easy. There were already thirteen godmothers in the family and there wasn't an aunt, a cousin, a neighbor, or a niece who was not already a godmother to one of the children. "Who will we ever find for Claudine?" they sighed.

The next morning an old lady arrived at the woodcutter's house riding on a stick as twisted as herself. Her gown was patched, her scarf moth-eaten, and her hair as wild as the weeds. "I heard that you are looking for a godmother," she said. "I would love to have your adorable child as a goddaughter."

"Who are you?" asked Antoine. "And where are you from? We can't have a godmother we don't even know! Out of here—and fast!"

"So that's the way it is, you ungrateful people. Well, you shall see who I am!" And she touched the little girl with the tip of her stick and shrieked, "You will become a frog and jump into the pond!" Claudine immediately disappeared from her cradle and a small "croak croak" could be heard from outside.

Antoine and Antoinette threw themselves at the feet of
the old woman who was none other than Grisnel the witch.
"For pity's sake, please return our little girl," they cried.

"That which is done cannot be undone," answered
Grisnel.

At this, the children ran to their parents and they all
began to cry. Grisnel drew back, her heart melting. "That
which has been done cannot be undone," she repeated. "I
cannot go back in time. But I can give you three wishes
to better the fate of your daughter."

Immediately Antoine said, "Get her out of that dirty
puddle in our yard."

"Done," said Grisnel. "She shall live in the beautiful
clean marsh nearby."

"Let her be able to speak," sobbed Antoinette.

"I will give her a human voice," said Grisnel.

"Let her marry a handsome husband," sighed the eldest
daughter.

"She shall, she shall," answered Grisnel.

Claudine was very happy in the marsh. She swam and dived in the clear waters.

She chased flies and rested in the cool green shade.
There were many frogs in the marsh and she had many friends.

From time to time, Claudine's parents and brothers and sisters came to visit her. She spoke to them of the delights of her life in the marsh. Her family spoke to her of their life in the village. But little that was told her had any meaning as she had left home much too young to have any memories of it. Soon her family stopped coming. Only the witch Grisnel came, for she had become quite attached to Claudine and thought of her as her granddaughter.

One day Claudine wandered away from the marsh and followed a little stream across the fields. She stopped to watch three men, a father and his two sons, cutting grass. As they stopped for lunch, the younger son, Charles, went to the stream to get the water bottle that was cooling there. It was then that he first saw Claudine, sitting on a stone, shimmering and sparkling in the sunlight. "Oh my, what an exquisite little creature," thought Charles.

After lunch and the afternoon's work, Charles lingered by the stream while his father and brother Leon started for home. He was surprised to see the little frog still sitting on the stone and said, "What! You are still here?"

Charles was astonished when the little frog answered, "Yes, I was waiting for you to return." And Claudine then told Charles the whole story of who she was and how she had come to be a frog.

Claudine, with her exquisite green-spotted brown skin, her delicate feet, and her golden eyes, was stunning and she appealed more and more to Charles. And it isn't every day that one meets a frog that can tell you the story of her life. So Charles asked Claudine to come and live with him in his little farmhouse. Claudine sang out, "Yes!" and hopped on Charles's shoulder to be carried off to her new home.

There Claudine had her own room in the attic
with a window so that she could always see the trees
and the sky. She also had her own tub with water
to swim and play in. Charles brought her juicy flies
and tender mosses and bread crumbs to eat.
Claudine was never happier, and one afternoon she
asked a passing swallow to tell Grisnel that she was
living happily with the man that she loved.

One day Charles's father fell ill. He called in his two sons and said, "I cannot divide my land between you. Each half would be too small to allow you a living. So I will leave all of the land to one of you and I will give the other enough money to allow him to learn a trade and work in the city. I love you both dearly and it is difficult to choose. So I have decided to leave my land to the one who will bring me a piece of canvas seven times longer than the tower of the house."

The next day Leon harnessed the donkey to the cart and went off to look for the piece of canvas. Charles went up to the attic of the little house where he found Claudine nibbling on a bit of moss and watching the puffy white clouds tumbling by the window.

"Ah, dear Claudine. I need a piece of canvas seven times longer than the tower of the house. Otherwise I cannot inherit my father's land and I will have to go live in the city and learn a trade. I would much prefer staying here, working in the open fields and taking a noon break with you under a rustling tree."

Claudine jumped onto Charles's shoulder. "I'll get you out of this. Wait here. I will be back by nightfall."

"Watch out for cart wheels and nasty children who put little frogs in jars!" cried Charles as Claudine hopped out of the window.

Claudine went to the forest and called Grisnel, who soon appeared riding on her stick.

"What do you want, my pretty little thing?" she asked.

Claudine told her about Charles's inheritance and the piece of canvas. Grisnel reached into a fold of her tattered dress and pulled out a golden box no bigger than a pear. "Take this, dear Claudine, and tell Charles to open it in front of his father after Leon returns." Claudine returned home and gave Charles the little golden box.

A week later Leon returned with his cart loaded with a huge roll of canvas. Unrolling it he grumbled, "It was the longest I could find."

Alas, it was only three times as long as the tower.

"And where is your piece of canvas, Charles?" asked his father.

Charles opened the box and inside was a tiny roll of canvas. He then unrolled it to exactly seven times the length of the tower.

"Bravo, my son. You shall inherit my land when you marry a good woman."

Charles was stunned. He rushed back to Claudine in the attic. "What good is it to inherit the land if I have to be separated from you," he cried.

Claudine's heart was full of sorrow.

"Listen," said Charles. "Go see Grisnel and ask her to put you into human form."

"That which is done cannot be undone," mumbled Claudine.

Charles slumped into a chair, his head in his hands.

Charles and Claudine sat for hours, their hearts breaking. There seemed to be no answer. Suddenly Charles leaped up.

"I have it, I have it! Let Grisnel turn
me into a frog! Then we can live together
happily ever after. Leon could get the
inheritance, and no one would miss me any
more than if I went to live in the city."
Claudine wept with joy.

Charles left a note on the kitchen table explaining to his father his reasons for leaving. Then he put Claudine on his shoulder, and off they went to find Grisnel.

Grisnel was delighted with the request and
she immediately touched Charles with her stick,
saying:

"Frog you will become,
Frog you will remain."

Charles and Claudine lived in the marsh happily ever after
and they had many beautiful and handsome little frogs.
And Grisnel was the godmother to each and every one.